Dr. Gardner's

FABLES FOR OUR TIMES

Dr. Gardner's
FABLES
FOR
OUR TIMES

RICHARD A. GARDNER, M.D.

Clinical Professor of Child Psychiatry
Columbia University, College of Physicians and Surgeons

Illustrations by
ROBERT MYERS

CREATIVE THERAPEUTICS

155 County Road   Cresskill, New Jersey 07626

Printed in the United States of America

10 9 8 7 6 5 4 3 2

Library of Congress Cataloging in Publication Data

Gardner, Richard A
    Dr. Gardner's fables for our times.

    SUMMARY: A collection of original fables, using
animals to illustrate human behavior, which could be
used with children to discuss their feeling about
and healthy modes of adaptation to showoffs, facing
fears, speaking one's mind, taking advice, and many
other aspects of conduct of concern to today's boys
and girls.
    1. Fables, American. 2. Children's stories,
American. [1. Fables. 2. Conduct of life—Fiction]
I. Myers, Robert E. II. Title. III. Title: Fables
for our times.
PZ8.2.G34Do   [Fic]   80-26098
ISBN 0-933812-06-X

To my daughter
Nancy Tara
My pride in you is unbounded

Other Books by Richard A. Gardner

The Boys and Girls Book About Divorce

Therapeutic Communication with Children:
    The Mutual Storytelling Technique

Dr. Gardner's Stories About the Real World, Volume I

Dr. Gardner's Stories About the Real World, Volume II

Understanding Children—A Parents Guide
    to Child Rearing

MBD: The Family Book About Minimal Brain Dysfunction

Psychotherapeutic Approaches to the Resistant Child

Psychotherapy with Children of Divorce

Dr. Gardner's Modern Fairy Tales

The Parents Book About Divorce

The Boys and Girls Book About One-Parent Families

The Objective Diagnosis of Minimal Brain Dysfunction

Dorothy and the Lizard of Oz

The Boys and Girls Book About Stepfamilies

Dr. Gardner's Fables for Our Times

Family Evaluation in Child Custody Litigation

Child Custody Litigation: A Guidebook for Parents and
    Therapists

Separation Anxiety Disorder: Psychodynamics
    and Psychotherapy

Acknowledgments

First, I wish to express my appreciation to the hundreds of child patients who have told me their self-created fables over the last twenty-five years. Their inspirations have served as the basis for the fables told herein.

I am indebted to Dr. Frances Dubner for having read the original manuscript and provided me with her wise advice. I am deeply grateful to my ever-loyal secretary, Mrs. Linda Gould, for her devotion to the typing of the manuscript in its various renditions. I am fortunate in having made the acquaintance of Mr. Robert Myers, whose illustrations so admirably complement the text. Lastly, I am deeply indebted to Mrs. Barbara Christenberry for her dedication to the editing of the original manuscript and then carrying it through the various phases of production to its final book form.

Contents

Introduction
for Adults

The survival of a social group has always depended on the implementation of measures designed to discourage and prevent individuals from exhibiting behavior that threatens the group's well-being and safety. A wide variety of social institutions have been utilized to serve this purpose. It is reasonable to assume that one such institution, storytelling, evolved in the following way.

We can speculate that hundreds of thousands of years ago, in many different societies, in various parts of the world, a leader of a tribe asked the members of the group to come out of their caves and/or trees to attend a special meeting. The leader could conceivably have said: "I've brought you all here to tell you that it has come to my attention that certain individuals have been observed to be engaged in behavior that is detrimental to the welfare of our group. For the safety and well-being of us all, it is crucial that such behavior cease. For example, you there, John, have been observed doing A, B, and C. We cannot allow such things to go on. Such actions create a state of fear in the rest of us and cannot be tolerated. Accordingly, if you do not discontinue such transgressions immediately, we will implement punishments 1, 2, and 3. And you there, Mary, have been engaged in antisocial behavior types D, E, and F (especially F). Again, such behavior cannot be tolerated if we are to remain a cohesive social organization. We cannot have among us individuals who engage in such behavior if we are to survive. Accordingly, if you are again found involving yourself in such activities, we will implement punishments 4, 5, and 6."

After a few more such public confrontations, the group was dismissed and told that such meetings should prove useful and that they would be periodically scheduled. Needless to say, it is not likely that the attendance at the next meeting was very high. Probably only the most masochistic individuals—those who seemed to thrive on public humiliation—attended the next gathering. Accordingly, the leaders must have concluded that such direct confrontations were not an effective method for bringing about a cessation of the undesirable behavior. "There must," they probably thought, "be a better way."

One better way probably evolved from an ancient and universal form of entertainment. Remember, prior to the twentieth century—and in many parts of the world to this day—there was little to do after the sun went down. There were not only no television sets (how did they possibly survive?), but no electric lights either. Especially in rural areas (which comprised the vast majority of the world prior to the twentieth century), it was pretty dark, to say the least. Fire, of course, was the main source of illumination—with the occasional addition of moonlight and starlight for the outdoor types.

Once there was a little fire light on the night scene, the next problem was that of what to do. Certainly there was work to be done—night and day—but what about recreation and diversions, those ancient antidotes to the boredom that must have been stultifying to all but the simplest? Perhaps telling about the events of the day could serve to liven up the place. But what was there to talk about? What could there be of burning interest in the events related to plowing a field, chopping wood, or picking fruit all day? Very little, especially if the recitation was confined strictly to the day's events. A little more interest could probably be evoked by talking about some minor event that was somewhat atypical. But if the relater did not mind expanding the truth somewhat, and if the listeners enjoyed fanciful elaboration (and were not sticklers for strict honesty), then the evening might be jazzed up after all. In this way the ancient tradition of storytelling—a tradition that is still very much with us—was probably begun.

14

Somewhere along the line, people must have realized that important social messages could be introduced into the story and woven into its fabric. Many must have appreciated that stories lent themselves well to being utilized as the vehicles for the transmission of values, moral principles, and other guidelines of human behavior. It is reasonable to assume that the aforementioned leaders who were looking for "a better way" realized that the very stories that everyone was telling at home all along might be just the thing that they were looking for. But before such stories could really be useful, an important element had to be introduced, namely, *disguise.* Direct confrontation had predictably turned everyone off—all but the most masochistic. But telling stories about things that happened to *others* appeared to be far more palatable. And the farther away and the more remote the "others" were, the less threatening the story was to the listeners. The important principle, however, could be retained. The lessons that were learned could still be transmitted as long as it was others, rather than present company, who had learned them. The essential precondition for such stories being useful was that the leaders had to take the position: "Of course, no one here would do such things—or even think such things—but it's interesting to hear about others who have engaged in such nefarious practices and what they have learned from their experiences and misdeeds." And the farther away the story's characters lived, the more remote they appeared to be from the audience, the less threatened the listeners were. Last, making the men handsome, the women beautiful, and introducing adventure, humor, sex, violence, and dramatization, added to the attractiveness of the vehicle and ensured greater receptivity to the messages—even those that were particularly unpalatable. The central philosophy of the method is well stated in a refrain from a song sung by Jack Point, the jester, in Gilbert and Sullivan's operetta *Yeoman of the Guard:*

> When they're offered to the world in merry guise
> Unpleasant truths are swallowed with a will—
> For he who'd make his fellow, fellow, fellow creatures wise
> Should always gild the philosophic pill!

Storytelling, in short, has proved to be one of the most powerful techniques that mankind has ever devised for molding human behavior. It is attractive and nonthreatening. It allows for the impartation of important principles and guidelines without the listener experiencing personal guilt or fear of incrimination. The listeners are usually not even consciously aware that their interest is dictated primarily by the fact that they harbor the exact same impulses (however unacceptable) as the story's protagonists, that they are grappling with the exact same conflicts as those who lived far away, long ago, in distant lands. The method is so powerful and useful that I would hazard the guess that it was crucial for the survival of the earliest civilizations and that those societies that did not utilize the method did not survive. Every society that I know of has its own heritage of such stories. These have been transmitted first by the spoken and then by the written word down the generations: the Bible, the Koran, various legends, myths, fairy tales, parables, fables, and other traditional tales.

The fable is one such vehicle. Like the others it utilizes symbolization in order to disguise. Like the others, it uses allegory to transmit its messages. Allegory, by definition, involves the representation of an abstraction via a concrete or material form. It is a symbolic narrative. And the fable is one of the purest forms of allegory. But the sine qua non of the fable is that its protagonists be animals. Without the animal, the story cannot justifiably be called a fable. An occasional human being may be found, but add too many and the story will no longer be a fable. But the animals in the fable are typically human, with all the human foibles: avarice, lust, jealousy, arrogance, false pride, and so on. Finally, the fable, if it is to be worthy of the name, has one or more morals or lessons. (It is nowhere written that a story must have only one moral!) Too many lessons may reduce a fable's effectiveness. Boggling the mind of the listener with too many is likely to lessen the impact of a single moral. (This danger notwithstanding, I found no less than 12 [yes 12!] lessons in one of my own fables, *The Pussycat and the Owl.*)

The use of the animal symbol for stories or other purposes dates back to the earliest civilizations. Animal drawings on

cave walls probably antedated human figures.
Anthropomorphization of animals is ubiquitous in primitive religions, animal worship being one manifestation of such anthropomorphization. (And anthropomorphization still persists in modified form in most modern and more sophisticated religions.) Children, who have much in common with primitives with regard to their thinking processes, are traditional lovers of animals. I am referring not only to the actual pleasure that children derive from animals in reality (from pets and visits to the zoo, for example), but to the use of animals as symbols in their fantasies. The animal appears to be the child's natural choice for allegorical symbolization.

Child therapists have known, since the second decade of this century, that children will tell them much about themselves if encouraged to relate self-created stories about animals. But try to get the children to appreciate that they are really talking about themselves, i.e., "gain insight" and they are likely to be turned off. This valuable source of information about their underlying psychodynamics may thereby be lost to the therapist. But discuss the animals as animals, and lengthy therapeutic conversations are possible. One 7-year-old child once said to me, upon being asked to make up a story about the animal figurines I provided him, "Remember, this story has nothing to do with me or anyone in my family. It's only about animals!" I agreed not to challenge him on this statement, and he was thereby allowed to provide me with a wealth of information about himself that was therapeutically useful. Had I tried to analyze his resistance to coming to terms with the fact that he was really talking about himself, I probably would not have been able to be of much help to him in the areas revealed by his story.

Without knowing that they have been doing it, children have been telling therapists fables for years (like the man who learns one day that he has been speaking prose since the earliest years of his life). Children are probably the best fabulists of us all. My experience as a fabulist comes via the Mutual Storytelling Technique in which I create stories that are modeled after the child's. After eliciting a self-created story from the child, I surmise its psychodynamic meaning and then create a story of my own, using the same characters (animal or otherwise) in a similar setting. But in my story, I introduce healthier modes of adaptation than those utilized by the child in his story. It was via experience with the Mutual Storytelling Technique, more than from any other source, that I came to create fables of my own.

Modern psychoanalytic theory provides us with a powerful tool for understanding the underlying meaning of children's stories, be they self-created fables or other symbolic narratives. It provides a depth of understanding far more profound than that which is generally appreciated by the listener. The same theoretical principles can be used in the creation of stories such as the fables I relate herein. But before reading them with children, the adult should realize that what happens to the animals in these stories and what they learn has *nothing* whatsoever to do with anything that has ever happened or will happen to anyone we know, child or adult.

Dr. Gardner's
FABLES FOR OUR TIMES

The Show-Off Peacock

As you may know, there are two kinds of peafowl, peacocks and peahens. The peacocks are the males, that is, the boys and the men peafowl. The peahens are the females, that is, the girls and the women peafowl. The peacocks are the ones that have long tails which drag around after them when they walk. The peacocks are the ones that can make a big fan by spreading out the feathers of their tails. The peacock's feathers are very beautiful and are mainly blue or green. The peacock

usually spreads his tail when an enemy animal bothers or tries to harm him. This lets the other animal know that the peacock will attack if the animal doesn't go away or will fight to defend himself if the other animal attacks him. The peahens, however, do not have such long feathers and cannot make the big fans that the peacocks can.

When the time of the year comes for peacocks and peahens to get together and make families of peafowl, one peacock usually lives together with from two to five peahens. The peacock then becomes father to all of the children that are hatched from all the eggs laid by the peahens in his family. The group of two to five peahens are called the peacock's *harem*. The word harem comes

from olden times in Arabia when the kings or sultans had many wives who were kept in a place called a harem.

Now that you have learned some important things about peafowl, I'd like to tell you about Peter the Peacock. He lived in the forest with many other peacocks and peahens. During the day he would play with the other peafowl. They would hunt for food on the ground. They would hop and jump, but not fly very much because peafowl do not fly very high or far. At night, however, they would fly up into the trees to sleep. It was much safer to sleep in the trees than on the ground.

When Peter was younger, he had many friends—both peacocks and peahens. Peter, like all of the other peacocks, had long colorful feathers. And as he grew older, they grew longer and more beautiful. Peter was especially proud of his feathers. They were bright blue in color and the bigger ones had a spot near the end that looked like an eye. When he would spread them in a big fan, it was a beautiful sight to see. He was so proud of his feathers that he started to spread them into a fan even when he didn't need to. The other peacocks only spread their feathers when they had to scare away enemies or let enemies know that they were ready to fight and defend themselves. But Peter would find every excuse to spread his feathers. He would sometimes even spread his feathers when very small animals were around, animals like chipmunks and rabbits. The other peafowl knew that these little animals weren't going to attack a big bird like a peacock. They knew also that Peter was just saying that these little animals were his enemies in order to have an excuse to show off his feathers.

After a while, Peter didn't even use the small animals as an excuse any more. He'd just spread his feathers and strut around saying to everyone, "Just look at my pretty feathers. Aren't they beautiful?" When he did this he thought that everyone was very impressed. He thought that everyone was admiring his feathers and thinking that he was very important. He didn't realize that such boasting and bragging just turned off the other peafowl. It really made everyone think that he was very conceited. It made the other animals think that he was more interested in himself and his feathers than anyone else. It made the other peafowl feel that the main thing Peter wanted from others was that they praise him and his feathers.

Soon, the other peafowl began calling Peter names like "big shot," "bragger," and "show-off." But Peter just thought that they called him these names because they were jealous of his feathers. He didn't want to accept the fact that those who called him these names were right, and that he was just what they were saying he was—a bragger and someone who was trying to be a big shot.

Time passed, and before long it came the time for families to form. Peter thought that all of the young peahens would want to be in his harem. To Peter's surprise, none of the peahens seemed to be interested. One peahen said, "I'm sorry, I've already promised someone else that I'll be in his harem." Another said, "Peter, you'll probably be more interested in your feathers than in me and the children. I don't want to be in your harem." And another peahen said, "All you want me for is to admire your feathers. I'm afraid that's all you'll want our children for as well. Sorry, Peter, I don't want to be in your harem." And another

said, "I don't like you Peter. You're just too conceited. I'd never want to be in your harem."

All this made Peter feel very sad and lonely. All around him new families were forming. Peter really had a fine set of feathers, but he was such a show-off that they brought him much more pain than pleasure. He was so conceited that they brought much more grief than happiness. Had he been more modest, and had he boasted less, he too would have had a harem like those that brought so much pleasure to the other peafowl.

Lessons:
1) Show-offs are disliked much more than they are admired.
2) If you are modest about the good things you have, you are much more likely to gain the admiration and affection of others.

The Kangaroos and their Pouch

Mother kangaroos usually have only one baby at a time. But once in a while, two kangaroos will be born at about the same time. This is what happened one day in Australia, the place where most of the kangaroos in the world live. On that day, both a boy and a girl kangaroo were born. The sister was called Koo and the brother was named Roo.

Because they were only little babies, they loved to stay in their mother's pouch. There it was warm and comfortable. And when they were hungry, all they had to do was suck at their mother's breasts, which were right in the pouch in which they lived.

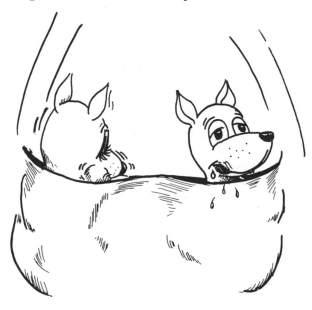

One day, just after they had finished their milk, their mother said, ''You children are getting older now. It's important that you spend less and less time in my pouch and more and more time outside. You have to learn about the world, both the good and the bad things that can happen in it.''

Koo was happy to hear the news. It meant to her that she was growing up. Roo, however, was sad. He loved

the warmth and comfort of the pouch and didn't want to leave it.

When the mother pulled Koo out of the pouch, she was scared at first, but she was very curious to see what the world was like. And so, even though she was frightened, she let her mother pull her out.

Roo was curious also, but he was mostly scared. And so when his mother tried to pull him out of the pouch, he just held on tightly and wouldn't move. He clung so tightly to the wall of the pouch, and cried so loudly, "I

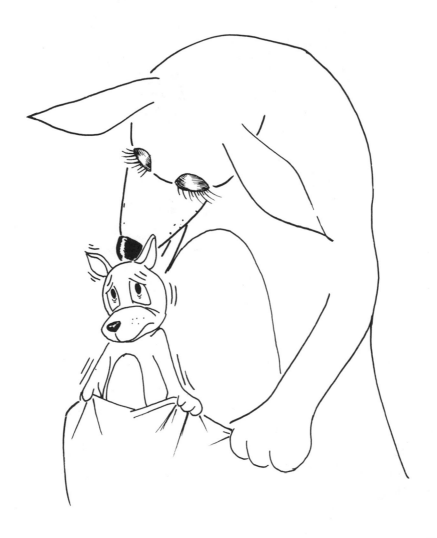

don't want to go," that his mother decided to let him stay.

In the meantime, Koo was having a fine time outside the pouch. She made some friends and was having a lot of fun. However, while playing with some of the other little kangaroo children, she fell and scraped her knee. She then hopped back into her mother's pouch.

When Roo saw his sister's scraped knee, he said, "I'm glad I didn't go out. Look what happened to you. You hurt yourself!"

"Yes, I did hurt myself a little," said Koo, "but I also had loads of fun. Even though I did hurt my knee a bit, I still want to go out and play again tomorrow because of all the fun I had."

"Well, you can do what you want," said Roo, "but I'm staying here where it's warm and comfortable and I can't get hurt."

And so the next day Koo went out and had a grand
time and Roo stayed in the pouch. As Roo was
snuggling inside his mother's pouch, he could hear Koo
and her friends playing. They were having a wonderful
time, jumping and dancing and singing and playing.
Roo then peeked out over the edge of the pouch to
watch them.

When Roo saw how much fun the other kangaroos
were having, he wanted very much to join them. But he

was also very scared. When his mother saw him looking
at the others playing, she said, "Why don't you go out
and play with the other little kangaroos?"

"I'd like to play with the other kangaroos and have
all the fun they're having," said Roo, "but I also like
this warm and cozy pouch."

"You can't have both at the same time," answered
his mother, "but you can have a little of each. You can

go out and play awhile and you can come back to the pouch later."

Roo knew that his mother was right. But he didn't know which to choose—the fun outside or the warm, cozy pouch.

"But I can get hurt out there," said Roo to his mother.

"Yes," she answered, "that can happen. But it will be more pleasure than pain. The two usually go together. If you don't take your chances with the pain, you won't be able to enjoy the pleasures."

Roo knew that what his mother said made sense, but he still didn't know what to do. He thought and thought for the rest of the day. And that night, he could hardly sleep wondering what to do.

The next day, Koo said, "Come on, Roo, let's go out together. You'll see how much fun we can have. And if you do get hurt, mother is still here to help. And if you get sad and lonely, you can still come back to the pouch."

And so Roo decided to take his sister's advice. He was very scared at first, but he finally got the courage to jump out. He was so scared that he was sweating all over and his knees were knocking, but he went out anyway.

Koo introduced Roo to all the other kangaroo children. At first, Roo was a little shy. But soon he felt

more comfortable. And before he realized it, he was having so much fun that he forgot about the pouch. And every day, it became easier and easier to leave the pouch. And the time came when he wasn't scared at all.

Lessons:
1) New things are scary, but each time you do them they become less frightening.
2) If you stay a baby, you'll miss out on all the fun big people have.

The Parrot and the People

Once there was a parrot. On the day that she was born, her parents decided that they wanted to give her a very popular name so that she would not be different from other parrots. They thought that it was very important to be the same as everyone else if one was to get along with other people. And so they decided to call her Polly which, as you know, is the most common name for a parrot.

When she was little, Polly, like all young parrots, would do or say things that her parents didn't like. At such times, her mother would say, "I'm glad no one else heard you say that. I'd be terribly embarrassed if someone heard what you just said." Or her father would say, "I'm glad Grandma and Grandpa weren't here to see what you just did. They'd be ashamed of you."

If Polly spoke too loudly, her mother would often say, "Keep your voice low. What do you think the neighbors would think if they heard you?"

And that was the thing that got Polly most upset, when her mother would talk about what the neighbors would think about what she did. Once Polly answered, "I don't care what the damn neighbors think."

To this her mother answered, "You horrible child. You'll disgrace us all."

Once, during an argument about the neighbors and what they would think, Polly said to her mother, "All you care about is what the neighbors think. What about *my* feelings? What about what *I* think?"

Again, her mother got very angry and answered, "If I didn't care about you, I would let you do and say anything. It's because I love you so much that I want to protect you from the neighbors' not liking you."

Another thing that Polly's parents taught her was that it was very important that she never do or say anything that would hurt other people's feelings. That seemed like fine advice. However, she was even taught that she should not give an opinion on a subject if that opinion might be different from another person's. She was taught not to express an opinion that might hurt another person's feelings. As she grew older, there were more and more things she was told not to discuss with others in order that other people would not get upset or angry about what she said.

Polly's father was a very hard-working man, but he didn't earn too much money. At times, there was barely enough food to eat. Polly's mother and father hoped that when she grew up she might become a pet in a human being's house. Then, she would be given food, water, and a warm place to live and she'd never have to worry about these things again. They told her that the best way to become a pet in a person's house was to say exactly what the human being said. For example, if a human being said, "Polly wanna cracker?" she should repeat the same thing: "Polly wanna cracker."

Polly asked her parents what would happen if after the human said, "Polly wanna cracker?" she answered, "No thank you. I'm not hungry."

Her mother answered, "Humans want you to say what they want to hear, not what you think or feel like saying. If you say what you really think, you're going to have a hard time finding a human being who will want you to be a pet in his or her home."

One day, Polly's parents took her to a pet shop. She was too young to be given to the pet shop for sale as a pet. They just wanted her to see what happened when people bought parrots. They wanted her to learn what were the correct things to say to be sure that she would be bought by someone who wanted a pet parrot. In the pet shop there were other parrots who were old enough

and ready to be sold. The owner of the store was
talking to these parrots on how to act and what to say
to people who were interested in buying them. She told
the parrots, "The people who'll be looking for pet
parrots will be coming soon. They usually like parrots
who talk. And they like best, parrots who repeat just
what they say. So if you want to be sold, it's best for
you to repeat exactly what they say."

The woman continued, "Humans like to call parrots
'Polly,' even if you're a boy. So it's best to answer to
that name. They like to say things like, 'Polly wanna
cracker?' So it's a good idea to say back, 'Polly wanna
cracker.' Just say exactly what they say and you'll have
a good warm home, with lots of food and water for the
rest of your life. If you say what you're really thinking,
especially something that they might not like to hear
you say, you're not going to be bought by most
people." And all the parrots nodded their heads in
agreement and started practicing, "Polly wanna
cracker. Polly wanna cracker. Polly wanna cracker."

Polly was very sad over what she had just seen. First,

she didn't like the idea that her name really was Polly. She didn't feel very special having the same name as most other parrots. And it made her feel angry at her parents that they had chosen a name that humans would like and probably did not even think about what name for her they themselves might like. She knew that if she told her parents these thoughts they would get very upset and angry and make a big fuss in the store. So she kept quiet.

Soon some people came into the store. They said that they wanted to buy a parrot and, just as the storekeeper had said, they started calling all the parrots by the same name, "Polly." And just as the storekeeper had said, they all said to the parrots, "Polly wanna cracker?" And the parrots who said it just the way humans say it, got bought. And those who said it in a different way, or those who said something else, or those who didn't say anything at all, didn't get bought.

As Polly went home with her parents, she was very sad. The idea that the best way to be loved by humans was to say just what they want you to say was very depressing. When they got home Polly asked her mother if she could change her name. "What's wrong with Polly?" said her mother. "It's a wonderful name. Why, it's the most popular name for parrots, and it's the parrot name that human beings like most of all."

"That's just it," said Polly. "I want a name that's different. And I want a name that I like, not what others like."

"Well," said her mother, "if you keep talking that way, you'll never be bought by a human being. If there's one thing humans can't stand it's someone who's different from the others. So you'd just better stop that kind of talk right now or I'll send you to your room without supper."

Polly remained quiet, but she went to her room anyway. There she lay down and started to cry. "When I get older," she said to herself, "I'm going to change my name. I'm going to call myself *Nancy,* whether other parrots or people like it or not. I like the name Nancy. And someday I'm going to use it. But I guess I'd better not say anything about that now, because everyone would just get angry at me."

Time passed and Polly started to go to school. There she learned how to read and write. She liked school very much and was a very good student. She did so well in school that when she got into the higher grades, they put her into an Honors Class. Only the best and most hard-working students were chosen to be in the Honors Class.

On the first day in the Honors Class, Polly's new teacher, Ms. Freed, said, "I like to call children by the names they *really* like to use. You know, when children are first born, they have no choice but to use the names that their parents have chosen for them. I think that's all right, because a newborn can't be expected to chose his or her own name. But when a child gets older, I think he or she should be entitled to decide which name to use. So if you like the names your parents have given you, fine. I'll call you that name. However, if you'd like to use a different name, I'd be happy to call you that."

Polly was very happy to hear this. She already knew that she was getting to like Ms. Freed. When her teacher came to Polly and asked her which name she would like, Polly answered, "My parents named me Polly, but I don't like that name. It's very common and the only reason they chose it was because they wanted a name that would please humans. I don't even think they thought of another name for me. I think they would have called me Polly whether I was a boy or a girl. I like the name Nancy very much. Although it's an unusual name for a parrot, I like it anyway. Besides, I once had a human babysitter named Nancy. She was very kind and very smart. I'd like you to call me Nancy.''

"Fine," said Ms. Freed, "I not only like your new name, but I think your reasons for choosing it are excellent.'' And so the teachers and all the other students in the class started calling Polly "Nancy." By the end of the day, she was already getting used to her new name. And as she went home from school that day, Nancy said to herself, "I like Ms. Freed very much. I think she and I are going to get along quite well.''

That evening, while Nancy was in her room, her mother called out from the kitchen, "Polly, please come here. I want to tell you something." Nancy didn't answer, even though she had heard her mother. "Polly, Polly, I'm calling you. Please come here." Again, she didn't answer.

"Polly, I know you're there. I know you can hear me. Now come here this minute," cried out her mother angrily. Again, Nancy didn't answer.

Finally, her mother came storming up into her room. "What's wrong with you, Polly?" said her mother. "Why aren't you answering me?"

"My name isn't Polly any more," answered Nancy. "It's Nancy!"

"Now what kind of a stupid name is that for a parrot?" screamed her mother. "What will everyone think of us, having a daughter with a name like Nancy?"

"I don't care what other people think," said Nancy. "It's the name I like and it's the name I'm going to use. I *hate* the name Polly and I'm never going to answer to it again."

When Nancy's mother told her father what Nancy had said, her father said to Nancy, "Polly, you'll never get bought by a human being if you don't listen to our advice."

"I'd like to be bought by a human being and be a pet in a human's home, but not if I have to be called Polly," said Nancy. "There must be some humans in the world who like parrots with names other than Polly."

Although her parents were very upset, they realized

that Nancy was getting older now and could make more and more of her own decisions. Therefore, they started to call her Nancy. But because they had called her Polly so long, they often forgot her new name and would often still call her Polly by mistake.

One day Ms. Freed told the class that during the next few weeks they were going to study all about human beings. Then, after a few weeks, she wanted everyone in the class to write a composition about humans. Nancy liked the whole idea and worked long and hard learning all about humans. Then, after a few weeks, she worked very hard on her composition. Nancy was very proud of the paper she had written and was sure that she would get a very high grade and a very good comment as well. Nancy couldn't wait to get her composition back from Ms. Freed.

Next week, Ms. Freed returned the students' papers. Instead of getting the A that she had expected, Nancy got a C minus. You can imagine how surprised she

was when she looked at her paper. And instead of getting a very good comment, Ms. Freed wrote, "Nancy, please see me after class." Nancy was so upset, she was ready to cry. She had to try very hard to hold back her tears. She didn't want to cry in front of everyone in the class, especially because she had been taught to believe that it was a shameful thing to cry, even if she was very upset.

Throughout the rest of the day, it was hard for Nancy to concentrate on what Ms. Freed was teaching the class. All she could think of was the composition, and why she had gotten a C minus. All she could wonder about was what Ms. Freed would have to say to her at the end of the day.

At last the school day was over and Nancy was finally going to find out what had happened with her composition. Ms. Freed began, "I know you're very upset with your grade, Nancy, and I hope that after you've heard what I have to say, you'll agree with me that I didn't make a mistake."

"Please tell me quickly," said Nancy. "I just can't imagine why you thought my paper only deserved a C minus."

"After reading your composition," said Ms. Freed, "it was clear to me that you had learned well all the things that *I* had to say about human beings in the classroom. It was also obvious that you had learned well all the things that *others* had written about humans in the books you read. But *no where* in your composition did I see one word about *your* opinion about human beings. I know, from the things you've said in class, that you have some definite opinions about humans—especially with regard to the fact that they have trouble dealing with people who are different. But you didn't write any of your opinions in your composition. Had you done so, I probably would have given you an A or even an A plus.''

Nancy could say nothing. She just sat there silently. She knew that what Ms. Freed had said was true.

Ms. Freed then continued, ''You see, Nancy, the best way to learn about something is to learn first about what others have to say about the subject—especially those who know more about the subject than you. It's always best to start by listening carefully to those who have taken the trouble to learn about the subject. Then, it's a good idea to think about what these people have to say. Decide for yourself what seems reasonable to you and what does not. You must be able to respect the opinions of others, but you must be able to respect your own opinions as well.''

Again Nancy could say nothing. She agreed that what Ms. Freed said made a lot of sense.

''What I have just told you is very, very important,'' said Ms. Freed. ''In fact, it's one of the important things a person can learn. I hope that you will remember this grade for a long time. If I had given you an A, I don't think you would have remembered as well all the important things I have just said.''

''You're right,'' said Nancy. ''The C minus hurts, but you're right. You are a very nice person,'' continued Nancy, ''and I love you.'' The two then hugged and Nancy left.

Nancy was crying again, but this time not out of sadness, but out of love and joy. She knew that she had learned a very important thing, something she hoped she would never forget.

When Nancy got home that day, her parents told her that she was old enough now to leave the home. They were going to bring her back to the pet shop and try to find for her a nice home with a human being. Nancy was sad at the news, but she knew that her parents were right, that she was now old enough to leave.

As she walked to the pet shop, Nancy's father suggested that she tell the owner that her name was Polly. "No way," answered Nancy. "My name is Nancy! There must be some human being in the world who likes the name Nancy for a parrot."

And, as they got close to the store, her mother said to her, "Remember, say just what the people want you to. Nothing else."

"I'll say what I want to," said Nancy. "Just because I'm a parrot doesn't mean that I don't have a mind of my own. There must be some human in the world who will like me even though I don't just repeat what he or she says."

When they got to the store, the woman who owned it asked Nancy what her name was. "Nancy," she responded.

"What an unusual name for a parrot," said the lady.

"Tough on you, if you don't like it," said Nancy.

"With an attitude like that, young lady, you're going to be sitting around here a long time," said the owner.

"That's fine with me," said Nancy. "I'd rather sit here than be in the home of some simple-minded human who can't stand anyone who's different or who has to be surrounded by those who say just what he or she wants to hear."

When the first customers came in, they went over and said to Nancy, "Polly wanna cracker?"

"The name is *Nancy,*" she replied.

"Nancy? What a funny name for a parrot. Sorry, we won't buy you. We want a Polly."

"That's tough," said Nancy.

Everybody got upset after Nancy said that—her parents, the storeowner, and the people who were planning to buy a parrot.

"I don't know if I'll be able to sell her," said the storekeeper to Nancy's parents.

"Please try," said Nancy's parents. "She's really a very fine parrot and she's very smart, as well."

"She's a spunky little thing. I'll have to admit that," said the storekeeper. "Since you're such nice folks, I'll keep her around for a while. But she's a tough one, let me tell you."

The next day some other people came into the store to buy a parrot. They went over to Nancy and, of course, said, "Say, 'Polly wanna cracker?'"

"You're in the wrong place," answered Nancy. "You don't want a bird, you want a phonograph record." And these people, too, got very upset.

And so, day after day, people came to the store and, although other parrots were sold, Nancy wasn't. No one wanted to buy Nancy. Everyone who came into the store was unhappy with a parrot named Nancy. They all wanted one named Polly. All the people wanted the parrot to say what they wanted it to say. No one wanted a parrot who had its own opinion about what to say and what not to say.

Finally, the storekeeper told Nancy that if she wasn't sold in a few days, she would have to return to the home of her parents. She was causing her to lose too many customers. As the storekeeper was telling this to Nancy, a customer who was standing nearby overheard the conversation. He told the storekeeper that he liked parrots very much, had a few at home, and had come to buy another. He thought Nancy was a nice looking parrot, and he couldn't understand why no one wanted to buy her.

"You just talk to her a few minutes," said the storekeeper, "and you'll see why."

So the man went over to Nancy and said, "What's your name, young lady?"

"If you're looking for a parrot named Polly, you're going to be very disappointed," answered Nancy. "My name's Nancy."

"Sounds like a very nice name to me," said the man.

"I hope you're not going to ask me to say, 'Polly wanna cracker' or even 'Nancy wanna cracker,'" said Nancy.

"There's nothing special I want you to say," said the man. "But what have you got against saying that you want a cracker?"

"There are two things," answered Nancy. "First of all, it's just repeating what someone else wants me to say for their amusement—not mine! I'm just not that kind of person. And second, I just don't like crackers."

"What would you like to say then?" asked the man.

"I'd like to get out of this stupid place once and for all," said Nancy, "and live with some intelligent people and parrots who have minds of their own."

"I have just the place for you," answered the man.

"Really," said Nancy. "Where?"

"My house," said the man. "I like parrots and I have a few at home. They are very independent types, just like you. They weren't easy to find either. Most parrots are so used to saying what others want them to say that they long ago stopped having opinions of their own. I think you'll like living in my house."

So the man bought Nancy and took her home with him. The storekeeper, as you can well imagine, was very happy to sell Nancy. But Nancy, as I am sure you will agree, was even happier to leave. When she got to the man's house, though, Nancy had the biggest surprise of her whole life. One of the parrots who lived

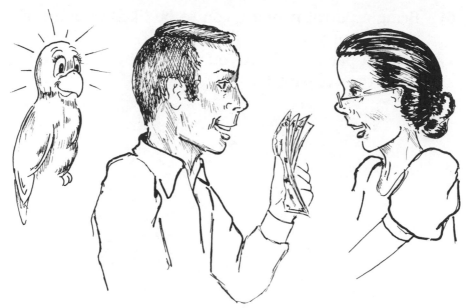

in the man's house was her good friend and teacher, Ms. Freed, the person who had taught her so many useful things. And that was the happiest moment of all.

Lessons:
1) Listen carefully and learn from those who seem to know what they're talking about.
2) Think for yourself and form your own opinions as well.
3) Don't believe everything everyone else says. Accept as true those things that others tell you that seem reasonable to you at that time. Do not accept those things that, in your own opinion, do not seem reasonable.
4) If you disagree with something someone else tells you, try to come up with a better answer yourself.
5) If you say things that most other people do not believe, you must be brave enough to take their criticism.

6) Being a parrot may get you to be liked by a lot of people, but you won't like yourself.
7) Being a parrot will get you disliked by those who don't respect parrots.

The Squirrels
and
the Skunk

One spring morning, two squirrels, Furry and Squrry, were playing in the forest. They were having a lot of fun. They didn't know that a skunk was watching them from the nearby bushes. The skunk saw how much fun the squirrels were having and wanted to play with them.

All of a sudden, Furry saw the skunk. He cried out, "Let's get away from here fast. If we don't run fast, he'll spray his smell on us."

"Please don't run away," cried the skunk. "I won't bother you. I promise."

"Don't run away so fast," said Squrry to Furry. "The skunk said he won't harm us."

"Don't believe him," said Furry. "Everybody knows that all skunks will spray you with a terrible smell."

"Wait," said the skunk. "It's true that all skunks *have* smells. But it's *not* true that we always *use* our smell."

"When do you use it?" asked Squrry.

"Only when someone tries to hurt us," said the skunk. "Our smell protects us from danger. It's so terrible that people and animals run away from it. So it's good protection against those who try to hurt us. We never use our smells with our friends. And I'd like to be your friend."

"It sounds like he won't use his smell on us," said Furry to Squrry.

"Especially if we don't try to harm him," said Squrry to Furry. "And I see no reason for us to want to hurt him if he doesn't harm us."

The skunk answered, "As I've said before, I don't want to hurt or bother you. I want to be your friend. And if you're nice to me, I'll never use my smell on you. I promise."

"I believe him," said Squrry to Furry. "Let's play with him." Furry agreed to see what would happen, but he was still a little scared. So the three of them played together. After they had played together a number of times, Furry was no longer frightened. He agreed that Squrry was right. They hadn't tried to hurt

the skunk and he didn't spray them with his smell. After that they had wonderful times together and remained friends for a long, long time.

Lessons:

1) Be friendly and you'll have friends.
2) You often get from others what you earn or deserve.
3) The attacker is the one who often brings his own misery upon himself.
4) Don't believe every bad opinion you hear about others. Find out for yourself whether it's true or false.

The Pussycat and the Owl

Once there was a pussycat. Her name was Kitty. She had big dark eyes and beautiful dark brown fur. It was very smooth and the children loved to pet her. She was always a very friendly pussycat and enjoyed doing nice things for other people. She was very hard working at school and so did very well there. In fact, she was one of the best students in her class. Because of these fine qualities, she was liked not only by cats but by many other animals.

One day, a cat named Tom came to live nearby. He had fine white fur with a few gray spots. He was very big and strong and could do many things better than most of the other cats. For example, he could jump much higher and farther than most of the other cats. He could do all kinds of tricks and used to practice long and hard. When he did his tricks, many cats and other animals would come to watch him. And everyone admired Tom for all the neat tricks that he could do.

One of the animals who came to admire Tom very much was Kitty. However, Tom hardly paid any attention at all to Kitty. When she stood in a crowd to

watch him do his tricks, she was sure that he never even noticed her. And if she was with him when there were fewer people around, he still didn't pay much attention to her. This made Kitty very, very sad.

One day Kitty and Tom were talking together with a group of cats. There was a gray cat there named Suzy, to whom Tom was paying a lot of attention. Suzy was in Kitty's class in school and was one of the poorer students. Also, she was a very quiet person and so she didn't have too many friends. But, for reasons that

Kitty couldn't understand, Tom liked Suzy much more than he liked her. And so she continued to be very sad.

On another day, Kitty overheard Tom talking to some of the other cats. They were gossiping about the various cats that they knew and they didn't know that Kitty was nearby and could hear everything they were saying. She was very curious to hear what they were saying, even though she was a little ashamed that she was listening in on their conversation. Suddenly, they started talking about her. One cat said that he admired Kitty very much because she was a very nice person as well as a good student. Tom then said, "Kitty's just a bookworm. All she does is study."

"That's not so," said one of the other cats. "She does many other things as well and is a very fine and giving person."

"Well, I still don't like her type," said Tom.

Kitty was very upset when she heard this conversation, but she was at least glad to learn why Tom didn't like her.

Kitty went and sat under a tree and started crying

about the situation with Tom. Above her, sitting on a limb in a tree, was Oliver, the wise old owl. He knew most of the animals very well and, over the years, had learned many useful things. Most of the animals respected him greatly for his knowledge and frequently sought his advice. Although his name was Oliver, everyone called him "Olly." Kitty didn't know that Olly was up there in the tree watching her. After a while, the owl looked down and said, "What are you crying about, young lady?"

Kitty was startled by the owl's voice and looked up. "Oh, it's you," said Kitty. "I didn't know you were there."

"Yes," said Olly, "I've been watching you for some

time now and was wondering what you're crying about so bitterly. If you'd like to tell me the problem, perhaps I can help you."

"I hope you can, old owl," said Kitty.

"I'd like to try," said the owl. "What's troubling you?"

"It's Tom," said Kitty. "I like him very much and he likes Suzy much more. I'm friendlier and more giving than Suzy and yet he likes her more. I'm harder working in school and a better student than she is and yet Tom likes her more. He told some of the other cats that I'm a 'bookworm' and that he just doesn't like my type. I keep thinking that there's something wrong with me."

"That's not necessarily so," said the owl. "Just because someone doesn't like you doesn't have to mean that there's something wrong with you. In fact, there are two possibilities when someone doesn't like you. First, the person is right and there is something wrong with you. Second, the person is wrong and there's nothing the matter with you. No one can be liked by everybody. Just as you don't like everybody, you can't expect everyone to like you. The fact that he likes Suzy more doesn't necessarily mean that there's something wrong with you."

"So what should I do if someone doesn't like me?" asked Kitty. "How can I know whether they're right or wrong?"

"First," said the owl, "you should ask yourself if *you* think the person is right or wrong about the thing he or she doesn't like about you. If you can't decide yourself, then it's a good idea to get advice from someone whose opinion you respect—someone like a parent, or teacher, or very good friend. The older you get the better you'll be able to trust your own opinion. The older you get the less you'll need to ask others to help you decide whether the person who criticizes you is right or wrong. Now what do you think about Tom's criticism? Do you think he's right or wrong? Do you think that you are a bookworm?"

"No, I'm not," answered Kitty. "I do like to study and I do work very hard at school. But I don't study so much that anyone would call me a bookworm. I spend a lot of time doing other things as well—things having nothing to do with books. I don't think I'm a bookworm."

"So," said Olly, "is Tom right or wrong in his criticism of you?"

"He's wrong," said Kitty.

"I agree with you," said the owl. "I've known you since the day you were born and I know about all the different things you do. I, myself, have never considered you to be a bookworm. Even though you aren't, Tom still doesn't like people who study a lot. You told me he said that he didn't like your type. Does that necessarily mean that there's something wrong with you?"

"I guess not," said Kitty. "Do you know that what you've just said is starting to make me feel better already."

Olly now flew down to the ground near Kitty. "There's more I can say about this kind of problem," said the owl. "When someone says they don't like something about you, you should not only ask whether they're right or wrong, but you should think about *who* it is who is criticizing you. Is the person someone whose opinion on the subject you respect? Or is it someone whose opinion is *not* worth taking seriously? Now what

about Tom? Do you respect his opinion on the subject of studying and bookworms?''

"Not particularly,'' said Kitty. "He never studies very much and doesn't seem to enjoy book learning. Therefore, he's not a very good student. In fact, he's one of the poorest students in the class—just like Suzy.''

"So he doesn't know very much about the pleasures one can get from book learning,'' said Olly.

"No,'' said Kitty.

"So do you respect his opinion on the subject?'' asked the owl.

"Not really,'' said Kitty. "You know, I'm feeling even better now that I realize that I didn't think about who the person was who was criticizing me. I didn't think about whether his opinion was worth taking seriously. And it certainly isn't.''

"I'm glad that that makes you feel better,'' said Olly. "Now there's one other thing you should ask yourself when someone criticizes you.''

"What's that?'' asked Kitty.

"You have to ask yourself, 'Why is this person criticizing me?' You have to think about whether the person is trying to be helpful to you or whether the person has some other reason for criticizing you. Now what do you think about Tom? What do you think might be his reasons for calling you a bookworm?"

"You know," said Kitty, "I had the thought yesterday that he might be jealous of me. But I quickly put that out of my mind and thought it was silly. I also thought that that wasn't a very nice thing to think."

"Well," said the owl, "I really can't know for sure what Tom is feeling but I think your guess is a good one. I think there's a good chance that he's jealous of you and that's why he calls you a name like bookworm. I think that there might be another reason, as well, for his liking Suzy more. And it also relates to school. Do you know what that might be?"

"I think he's more comfortable with her," said Kitty, "because she's not such a good student. So when he's with her he doesn't feel bad about himself for how little book learning he has. She doesn't have very much book learning either."

"Again, I don't know exactly what's going on in Tom's mind," said Olly. "However, I'm in complete agreement with you that what you say is probably true. He probably feels more comfortable with Suzy because she's at the same level as he is in the class. He's probably uncomfortable with you because you know much more about many other things than he does."

"You know," said Kitty, "I'm very happy I spoke to you. I really don't feel that bad any more about Tom's not liking me. I see now that, first of all, his reason for not liking me is wrong. I'm not the bookworm he thinks I am. Secondly, I see now that he's not someone whose opinion I really respect on this subject. I respect his opinion on gymnastics and on doing tricks, but not

on the subject of book learning because he knows very little about it. And lastly, I see now that his reasons for criticizing me probably have nothing to do with any faults of mine. He probably criticizes me because he's jealous of what I know, and he probably likes to be with Suzy more because he's more comfortable when he's with her. She doesn't know much about book

learning either so he doesn't have to feel bad about himself when he's with her. He doesn't have to feel bad that she knows more than he, because she doesn't. I guess that when he's with me, he feels embarrassed that he hasn't learned as much in school as I have.''

"It seems to me," said the wise old owl," that you've learned some very useful things this afternoon. And I'm very glad you're feeling better now."

"I've learned many important things today and I'm very grateful to you for what you've taught me," said Kitty as she started to leave.

"There's one other thing I'd like to ask you, before you leave," said Olly.

"What's that?" asked Kitty.

"What do you think you're going to do about all this?" said Olly. "Learning serves little if any purpose if we don't make use of what we learn."

"Well," said Kitty, "I guess I've just got to accept the fact that I can't have Tom as my boy friend."

"That's right," said Olly. "It's very important to know which things in life you can control and which things you can't. It's very important to be able to

decide whether something is controllable or not.
Knowing the difference between the things you can
control and the things you cannot is very, very
important. Then you should stop trying to change
things you can't change, but you should try to change
the things that you can."

"And Tom's liking Suzy is something that I cannot
control," said Kitty. "It's something I really can't
change."

"I agree with you," said Olly. "It certainly looks like
one of the things you have absolutely no control over.
So what are you going to do?"

"I'm going to try to find someone else who'll like me
more," said Kitty. "Looking for someone else is
something I can control. It's something I can do
something about," said Kitty.

"That's an excellent solution to the problem," said Olly. "Tom's not the only boy in the world. There are many other cats around here who, I'm sure, would like very much to be your boy frined. And they're more likely to show their interest in you if they learn that you're no longer hooked on Tom."

"You're right," said Kitty. "I think now that I'll be able to find someone else—a substitute. Then I'm sure it'll be much easier for me to forget about Tom."

And so Kitty went home. Her conversation with Olly had lasted a long time and it was getting very late. That night she thought a lot about the things that she and

Olly had discussed. She realized that she had learned some very useful and important things. But she didn't just *think* about what to do, she *did things* to make her feel better. She stopped spending time watching Tom do his tricks. Instead, she spent time with other cats. And, after a while, she met a new cat whose name was Andrew. He, like Kitty, was a very good student and they had a lot of things to talk about. He also was a very giving person and Kitty admired him very much for this. And so she and Andrew became very good friends and she was no longer sad about Tom. In fact, she hardly ever even thought about him again.

Lessons:

1) If someone doesn't like you, there are two possibilities. The person is right and there is something wrong with you. Or, the person is wrong and there is nothing wrong with you.

2) If someone doesn't like you, it's a good idea to try to find out the reason why the person doesn't like you.

3) If the person has a good reason, that is, if the criticism is right, then try to change the thing that is turning the other person off.
4) If the person has a bad reason, that is, if the criticism is wrong, then try not to take the criticism seriously.
5) If someone criticizes you, ask yourself whether the person knows enough about the subject to be taken seriously.
6) If the person should be taken seriously, then try to correct the problem.
7) If the person should not be taken seriously, then try to ignore the criticism.
8) If someone criticizes you, try to find out why. Is the person trying to be helpful? Or does the person have other reasons for criticizing you which have nothing to do with trying to be helpful to you.
9) If the person is really trying to help you, then try to change the things that cause the criticism.
10) If the person has other reasons, reasons which have nothing to do with being helpful to you, then try not to take the person seriously.
11) It's very important to try to learn the difference between those things you can control and those things you cannot control. It's very important to try to change the things that you can change and not try to change things that you cannot.
12) If you can't have something that you want very much, don't keep trying to get what is impossible. Try to get a replacement or substitute. Then you won't feel bad about not having gotten what you originally wanted.

The Wise-Guy Seal

A circus owner was going to need a new seal to perform tricks. One of his seals, who had worked for many years, was very old and wasn't going to be able to work very much longer. And so the owner put up a sign: "Wanted: A seal who can do tricks. The seal

who can do the best tricks will be chosen. Those who want to try out for this job should come to the circus two weeks from next Friday."

As soon as the sign was put up, most of the seals were very excited. Many of them wanted nothing more than to work in a circus and do tricks in front of hundreds, and even thousands, of people. And so those who wanted the job started to practice very hard. They spent hours balancing balls on their noses.

They leaped out of the water as high as they could in order to catch a little fish held by the trainer.

Some leaped through circles called hoops. And some even jumped through hoops that were burning with flames.

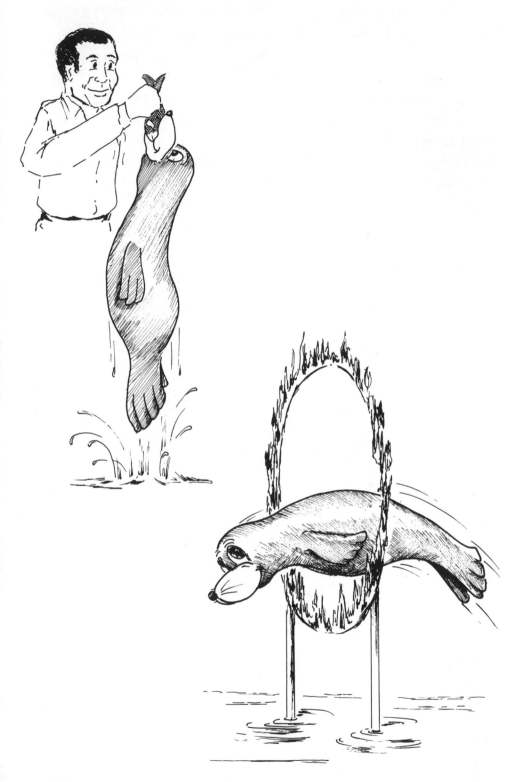

Sam, like all the other seals, wanted the job very much. Sam had learned many tricks too. But he was a wise-guy. He was so sure that he'd get the job that he didn't think that he had to practice. And so, while the other seals were spending most of their time practicing, in order to improve, Sam just swam around in the water having fun. Sam was sure that he could get the job without having to do all the work involved in practicing his tricks. Day after day the others practiced. And day after day Sam just relaxed, quite sure he was good enough to get the job.

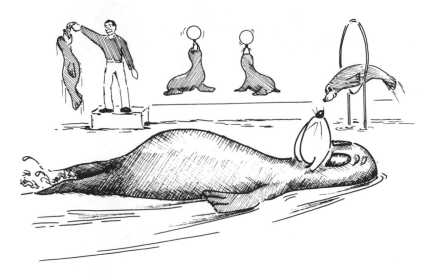

When other seals asked Sam why he wasn't practicing, he replied, "Aw, I don't have to practice. I'm good enough to get the job without going to all that trouble."

"You're just a wise-guy," said one of the others.

"With an attitude like that, you're in for a big disappointment," said another.

But Sam didn't listen. He just laughed at the others and said, "No one does tricks better than Sam. I've nothing to worry about."

Finally, the day came when all those seals who
wanted to try for the job had to come to the circus.
Dozens of seals were there. Each seal was asked to do
his or her best tricks. Some of the seals were so good
that the circus owner knew it was going to be very hard
for him to choose the best one for the job.

When Sam's turn came, the circus owner knew that
he wasn't going to have a problem deciding about Sam.
Sam did so poorly that everyone started to laugh. Sam
couldn't balance the ball on his nose for more than a
few seconds.

He couldn't jump high enough to take the fish out of the trainer's hand.

When he tried to jump through the hoop, he missed it entirely. Because of this, the circus owner wouldn't let Sam even *try* to jump through the flaming hoop. He feared that Sam might get burned.

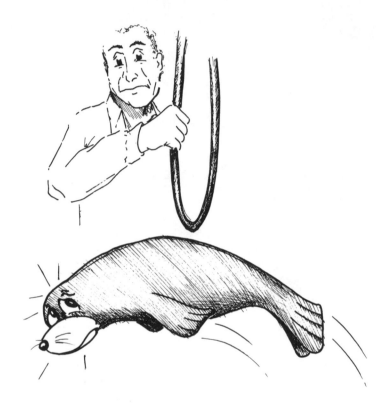

And so Sam didn't get the job. It was a very sad day for him—but in his heart he knew that the circus owner was right. He hadn't worked to keep up his skills, so he really didn't deserve the job.

Lesson:
No one is so good that he can't use some practice.

The Dogs and the Thieves

Once there were two dogs. They were brothers and they were born on the same day. They had five puppy sisters who were also born on that day. Because their mother's owner could not keep seven dogs, he decided to sell some of them a few weeks after they were born.

Fortunately for the two brothers, they were sold to families that lived right next door to one another. Although they missed their mother very much, they had one another to play with and so it was easier for them to get used to being without her.

Even though they were brothers, they were very different from one another. One was always barking, so the children with whom he lived decided to call him "Barky." The other dog was a happy and frisky little

fellow. He was very lively, so the people with whom he lived decided to call him "Sparky." Sparky hardly ever barked, but when something happened to make him

angry, he would growl softly. This warned those who bothered him that they'd better stop.

Both of the dogs' owners had bought them because they wanted their children to have pets. In addition, they hoped that the dogs would make good watchdogs and would scare away robbers and anyone else who might want to harm any members of the family.

As time passed, Barky barked more and more. He barked over every little thing. Sometimes he barked when something bothered him, like when he was hungry, or thirsty, or when he wanted someone to take him out to walk. Other times he would bark and no one could figure out why he was barking. No one had bothered him and he had just eaten a good meal and had just taken a walk. So the people in the family just

said, "Don't mind him. He barks so much that he doesn't even know what he's barking about. He often just likes to hear himself barking." And so people just got used to his barking most of the time and learned to ignore it.

Sparky was a much quieter dog. When he was hungry, he would sniff at the cupboard where the dog food was kept and he would smack his lips and teeth with his tongue. Then the family knew that he was hungry and they gave him some food. When someone did something to make him angry, Sparky would growl and sometimes he'd even make hissing sounds. He would pull his body back as if he were ready to leap upon and bite the person who was bothering him. That was usually enough to scare away whoever tried to make trouble for Sparky or anyone in his family.

It wasn't long before everyone in the neighborhood where the two dogs lived got to know about Barky. They got to know about him because of all the noise he made. But no one was afraid of him. People used to say, "Don't be afraid of him. His bark is worse than his bite." In fact, Barky never bit anyone. He was really afraid to bite, even when he was bothered or attacked. He just hoped that his loud bark would scare people away. Although people in the neighborhood knew Sparky, they didn't know much about him because he was a very quiet dog.

One day the mayor of the town announced that there was going to be a big party. The town was one hundred years old, and everybody was going to celebrate this big event. Practically everyone in town planned to go. There were going to be fun and games for the adults, as well as the children, and there was going to be a big parade. Everyone was very excited, especially the children, because they heard that there were going to be real clowns there, as well as prizes for those who won races and games. The children started to count the days until the celebration, and as the day came closer they became ever more excited.

Well, the day of the big celebration finally came. Of course, both Sparky's family and Barky's family went. But the dogs had to stay home in order to guard the houses. Both families knew that the day of the celebration would be a perfect one to rob houses because thieves would know that practically no one was staying home and practically everyone in town was going to be at the big party. But Barky and Sparky weren't very sad, as you might have thought, because they didn't know about the celebration anyway. They didn't understand where everyone was going. And so they were just a little lonely, but didn't realize how much fun they were missing.

When the children got to the celebration they were so excited that they started jumping up and down. There were bands, tents, games, clowns, magicians, and acrobats. They sold hot dogs, pizza, ice cream, and all other kinds of foods children like to eat. There were people who were dancing and singing. Everyone was having a great time. Everyone was having such a great

time that hardly anyone thought about what might be happening back at their homes.

Well, there were three bad teen-agers who lived in the town. And they knew that practically everyone would be at the celebration. They were such bad boys that it didn't even make them feel guilty, or bad about themselves, when they would steal other people's property. They didn't think about how terrible a person would feel when his or her property was stolen.

And so they decided to rob some houses while almost

everyone was at the big party. As they were walking down the street where Sparky and Barky lived, the first house they came to was Barky's. When they got to the back door, they could hear Barky starting to bark. "Don't worry about him," said one of the boys to the others. "There's nothing to be afraid of with this dog. His bark is worse than his bite. In fact, everyone knows he's scared to bite anyone."

And so the three boys broke the back window of the house and climbed in. Of course, when they got inside, Barky kept on barking loudly, but the boys just ignored him. And Barky didn't do anything else but bark, and bark, and bark. "You're right," said one of the other boys. "He's all bark and no bite." The boys started going through the drawers of the house and collecting

things in bags. They took silverware, jewelry, money, watches, and other precious things. Barky kept barking and the boys kept stealing.

While all this was happening, an old lady, who lived across the street, heard the barking. Of course, she just said to herself, "Oh, that's just Barky again. That dog never seems to stop barking." Had she known what was really happening, she would have certainly called the police. But because she was used to hearing Barky's bark so often, she didn't think that his barking was a signal that there was trouble, and she didn't pay any more attention.

And so the boys took all the valuable and precious things they could find and climbed out of the back window of Barky's house. As they left, they started laughing about how easy it was. They especially laughed at Barky, who was indeed, "all bark and no bite."

Next they decided to break into Sparky's house. As they got closer to the house, Sparky heard them and ran toward the place where they were. As they looked into the back window, they saw Sparky inside. "Don't worry about him," said one of the boys. "He's the

brother of the dog next door." The other boys agreed, and they broke the window and started climbing in.

When they got into the house Sparky started snarling. One of the boys began to get scared, but the other two called him "chicken." The three of them started to

open drawers and closets. Then Sparky started to bark.
The boy whom the others had called "chicken" said,
"We'd better get out of here fast." But the other two
started to laugh at him and continued to search the
house.

While this was happening, the old lady across the
street heard the barking and said to herself, "If Sparky
is barking, there must be something wrong over there."

While she was calling the police, Sparky suddenly bit

the leg of one of the boys and held on as tightly as he
could. The boy yelled louder than he ever had in his
whole life. One of his friends started to run away and
the other tried to help him get Sparky off his leg. But
when the boy pulled Sparky off his friend, Sparky
started to bark at and bite *him*. There were such

terrible noises coming from the house, with the boys'
screams and the dog's barking, that the police had no
difficulty finding the house where all the trouble was.

   As they arrived at the house, the police caught the
boy who was trying to run away. He had only gotten
halfway down the block when the police came. All the
boys were then taken to the police station. One
policeman went over to the celebration, found both
families, told them what had happened, and brought
them to the police station. The parents of the teen-agers
were also brought down to the police station.

   Barky's family, of course, got back all their
possessions. But Barky was very ashamed of himself.

Sparky, on the other hand, was very, very proud. If not for him, the boys would have gotten away with all of his family's valuable possessions. People said that Sparky was like the kind of man who "speaks softly, and carries a big stick," that is, he doesn't make a lot of noise, but when there is trouble he can be counted upon to act with courage.

Lessons:
1) When a dog has a bark that's worse than its bite— everybody soon gets to know it!
2) Some dogs—like some people—"speak softly and carry a big stick." When they say or do something, it counts.

The Ant
and
the Grasshopper

Once there was an ant. His name was Andrew, but his friends called him Andy. He lived in a place called a colony. Andy's colony was under a rock so it couldn't easily be seen by the ants' enemies. The colony had a big central space and many tunnels all around for the

ants to go in and out. In the colony was the big queen ant, who gave birth to all the baby ants. The queen was the only female ant who lived in the colony. All the other ants were males. There were worker ants, who worked together to build the colony from twigs and nectar from plants that they used as glue. They also gathered food, like seeds and mold. And there were soldier ants, who worked together to defend the colony from enemies.

One day, Andy decided to take a walk—all alone. The queen ant had warned all the ants not to leave the colony alone. She said there were many large insects outside who like to eat ants. "If you want to go outside the colony," she said, "go in groups. In that way you'll be able to protect one another." But Andy didn't listen. It was very crowded in the colony, and Andy just felt like being alone for a while. He was sure that he'd be safe and that no one would bother him. And so he left the colony through a tunnel that opened near the edge of the rock that was above it. When he got out, he saw that it was a beautiful day. The sun was shining and the sky was a bright blue color. A few pretty, fluffy clouds floated in the heavens. Andy was happy to be alive and he walked briskly in the sunshine.

Suddenly, Andy saw a big grasshopper coming toward him. Now you may think that a grasshopper is not very big. In fact, you probably think that a grasshopper is very small. But, if you were the size of an ant, you would have a very different opinion. You would think, I am sure, that a grasshopper is a very big insect indeed. Anyway, Andy got scared and started to run back to his colony for help. He was then very sorry that he hadn't listened to the queen's warning and advice. Although Andy was a very fast runner, the grasshopper could leap in big spurts. And so the grasshopper got closer and closer. Andy was very, very scared. He knew that if the grasshopper caught him, he would be eaten up very quickly because grasshoppers love to eat ants. He knew, also, that if he could make

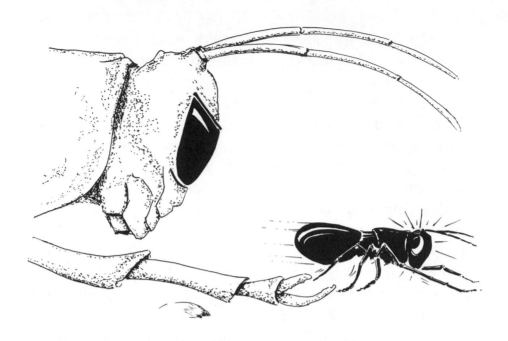

it back alive to his colony, his life would not only be
saved, but the grasshopper herself might be the one
who would be eaten. You'll see very soon why he
thought that.

Andy got back to the entrance to the tunnel of his
colony just a little ahead of the grasshopper. Andy
quickly crawled into the tunnel. And the grasshopper
crawled in after him. Without looking to see where she
was going, the grasshopper dived into the hole. She was
so anxious to get Andy that she didn't think about
what might be in the tunnel. She didn't even bother to
look down into the entrance. Had she done so she
would have seen all the ants down there and wouldn't
have dived in after the ant. Before the grasshopper
knew what was happening to her, many of Andy's
relatives swarmed around the grasshopper. Within a
few minutes they were all over the grasshopper's body.
The grasshopper tried to get out of the hole, and the
ants tried to pull her back. Although she was much

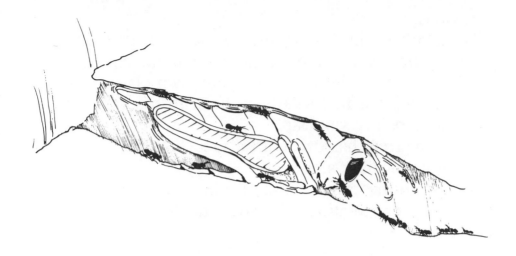

stronger than one single ant, all of the ants pulling
together were as strong as the grasshopper. The
grasshopper was scared that all the ants together would
eat her up. But finally the grasshopper was able to pull
herself out of the hole. She then leaped up into the air
and made the biggest hop of her whole life. Although
some of the ants still clung to her, with each hop, more
and more ants fell away. And she finally escaped.

You see, the grasshopper didn't know that Andy
wasn't just an ordinary regular ant. Andy was an *army
ant*. Army ants are famous for working together in
large numbers called *teams*. They are also famous for
their cooperation with one another. This is called *teamwork*. What one could never do alone, can be
accomplished by large groups. Sometimes army ants
work in groups of a few hundred ants. Sometimes there
are a few thousand. And there can even be groups of a
few hundred thousand! That, I am sure you will agree,
is a very large number of ants. In fact, there have been
groups of army ants that have eaten up animals as large
as a chicken or pig—so much power do they have
because of their teamwork.

Lessons:

1) Don't be quick to ignore the warnings and advice of those who are older and have more experience.
2) Don't jump into dark and unknown places without finding out first what's in them. In other words, look before you leap.
3) The group has strength far greater than that of each member alone.
4) When the group works together—as a team with good cooperation—this strength can be put to use.

The Dolphin and the Shark

Once there was a dolphin. Her name was Donna. In the part of the sea where she lived with her family, there were many other kinds of fish. One of the other kinds of fish were sharks. And one of the sharks was named Sharpy. He was called Sharpy because his teeth were very sharp and pointy. Sharpy wasn't just a regular shark. He was the kind of shark that's called a *great white shark*. Great white sharks are among the most dangerous animals that live. Of all the animals, human beings probably fear the great white shark the most. Many men have been eaten alive by these sharks. Because of this, they are sometimes called *killer sharks*.

Once in a while Donna and Sharpy would play together. But they hardly ever played together for very long because Sharpy would get very rough and then Donna would swim away. Or Sharpy would suggest that they have some fun by doing things that Donna thought were cruel or might get them into trouble. And Donna didn't want to get involved. For example, once Sharpy said to Donna, "I've got a great idea. Let's chase those people in the sailboat over there. As soon as they see my fin following their boat, they'll really get frightened. I'm not hungry, so I'm not going to eat them or anything like that. It'll just be fun to watch them panic. Just for laughs.''

Donna answered, ''That's a very cruel thing to do. Don't you have any feelings for others? Don't you care at all for them? Besides, don't you think they might do something dangerous to you? I know that if I were in their position, I'd want to do something very cruel to you for doing such a terrible thing to me. I'm sure you wouldn't like to be scared by others. If you think about how they'll feel, maybe you'll change your mind.''

Sharpy answered, ''Donna, you're no fun at all.

Besides, they can't do anything to me. It's just a sailboat.'' And then Sharpy swam toward the boat, leaving Donna behind. When Sharpy got near the boat, he started to swim directly behind it. He swam just below the surface of the water so that his fin would easily be seen sticking out of the water. He knew that it wouldn't take long before the people on the boat saw him. And he was right.

Suddenly one of the people on the boat yelled, ''Shark. Shark. Right behind the boat there's a shark!''

The other people on the boat started screaming, ''My God, a shark.'' ''What will we do? A shark.'' ''We'll all be killed.'' ''A shark. Do something please!''

When Sharpy heard all this, he started to laugh as

hard as he could. Seeing all these scared people was one of the funniest things that had ever happened to him. He then decided to swim even closer to the boat, just to get the people even more frightened. "He's coming closer," yelled someone. "He's going to go right under the boat."

"Oh, my God," yelled someone else. "What are we going to do?"

Just as Sharpy got so close to the back of the boat that he was practically touching it, he suddenly felt a sharp object hit him right on the top of his head. It was very painful. Then, just as he ducked, he heard a very loud noise. He quickly looked up and saw the sharp blades of a big motor spinning very, very rapidly.

Sharpy had not thought about the possibility that this sailboat, like many sailboats, might carry a motor that could be dropped into the water when there is too little or no wind. But now the motor was being used for a different purpose. It was being used as a weapon against Sharpy. Some smart woman on the boat had waited until Sharpy had gotten very close to the back of the boat and then quickly thrust the motor into the

water. She hoped that the blow would stun Sharpy and that the blades would cut into him. She hoped to kill him, or at least injure him so badly that he couldn't follow them.

Sharpy was lucky that he had quickly ducked so that the only thing that happened was that he'd gotten a few cuts on the skin of his head. And before Sharpy knew what was happening, the boat started speeding away very quickly. Sharpy didn't think about whether or not he could swim fast enough to catch up to the boat. He just wanted to go back home and rest and forget about the whole thing.

The next day, when he saw Donna, she asked him about the cuts on the top of his head. Sharpy told her what had happened. And Donna said, "I hope you've learned your lesson."

"I sure have," answered Sharpy. "Next time I'll be sure to choose a boat without a motor. Or, if it does have one, I'll be sure not to swim near the motor when I bother the people."

"It's too bad that that's the lesson you've learned," said Donna. "I hoped that you would have learned something about other people's feelings and that you can't do things like that without getting yourself into trouble."

Sharpy hardly listened to what Donna was saying because he was already thinking about new adventures. And, as he swam away, he thought about new ways to have fun. He also got very angry at human beings for the cuts on his head and the narrow escape he had had with the motor. He didn't think about the fact that he was being cruel and that he had brought this trouble upon himself.

As Sharpy was thinking about what else he could do, he suddenly saw another boat. It was a very small boat, with only two people on it. He knew that it didn't have a motor. Because he wasn't very hungry, he decided that he wasn't going to eat anyone. He just thought it would be fun to follow the boat awhile, scare people, and then get under the boat and turn it over. Watching the people splashing in the water, scared that Sharpy would eat them, would be great adventure.

So once again Sharpy swam with his fin high in the water so that the people would see him. And, sure enough, one of the people spotted Sharpy swimming right behind the boat. Immediately a man yelled, "Shark. There's a shark following us!"

The woman with him quickly picked up her special radio and called for help. "Hurry," she said into the microphone, "There's a shark following us. We're

about one mile north of the tower. Please send help quickly. I think it's a killer shark. Please help us!''

Sharpy didn't know that the people had sent for help. He thought that he had plenty of time to scare the people before tipping over the boat. So he just swam around the boat, getting ever closer. The closer he got, the more frightened the people became and the more Sharpy laughed. He didn't know that their cries for help were not only screams of fright, but were going into the radio as well.

Then Sharpy decided that he had had enough fun making the people scream and that it was time for even greater adventure. And so he began swimming toward the boat in order to tip it over. He was so interested in doing this, that he didn't hear the motor boats coming to help the two people. Then, Sharpy swam under the boat and, with a sudden lurch of his body, he knocked the boat over and the two people dropped into the water. They were screaming loudly and were petrified. They kept yelling, ''Help! Help! Help!''

Just then the two motor boats arrived. The people on them had guns and they started shooting at Sharpy. All of this came as a total surprise to him. He had certainly not expected this. Loud noises scared him and he suddenly felt a sharp pain in his tail. He had been hit by a bullet. Sharpy then knew that he'd better get out of there as fast as he could. He decided to dive very deep in the water, because he knew that the boats couldn't follow him down to the bottom of the ocean.

As Sharpy swam down into the depths of the sea, the

people with the guns picked up the man and the woman in the water. The two people, of course, were very relieved that they had been saved. They thought that Sharpy would certainly have eaten them. They didn't know that he was just having a little fun at their expense.

When Sharpy saw Donna the Dolphin the next day, she asked him how he got the hole in his tail. Sharpy

told her the story. Donna then said, "Again you've done a very mean thing. You deserve what you got and you're lucky they didn't kill you. I hope you've now learned your lesson, that you can't be cruel to people and expect nothing to happen in return."

But Sharpy was too angry to hear what Donna was saying. All he could think of were the cuts on his head, the motor that had almost cut him up, and the painful bullet hole in his tail. Now he thought that he had a very good excuse for hurting human beings. Now, he was not just going to bother and hurt them for fun, he was now going to do it for revenge. He was now going to do it to get back for what they had done to him. He was so interested in getting revenge that he didn't think about the fact that it was *he* who had started all the trouble in the first place. "I'll get back at them for what they've done to me," said Sharpy as he swam away. And he didn't want to hear any more advice from Dolphin Donna.

A few days later Sharpy said to Donna, "I've thought of a good way to get back at people for what they've done to me. Let's swim over to the beach where those people are swimming. I'm not particularly hungry, but it'll be a lot of fun to watch them all run out of the water when they see us coming. It's really fun to see how human beings get scared whenever they see my fin sticking out of the water. And it's even more fun when there are lots of people. And if you, Donna, jump high out of the water as well, and make a lot of splashing sounds, that will get them scared also."

Donna answered, "Sharpy, you're very, very cruel. Don't you have any feelings at all for others. Can't you imagine how terrible it will be for those people when they see a shark, especially a great white shark, coming up the beach toward them?"

"I'm not going to eat them," said Sharpy. "I'm just going to scare them. It'll make me feel good to get back at humans for what they've done to me. And besides, it's only fun."

"You seem to forget, Sharpy," said Donna, "that it was you who started all this trouble with people in the first place. Each time you've been cruel, you've gotten hurt. Yet you still haven't learned a lesson.''

Sharpy was so anxious to get back at the people and to have the fun of scaring them that he didn't hear a word of what Donna was saying. Then Donna said, ''Sharpy, I'm not going to join you in scaring those humans. They've done nothing to hurt me so I'm not going to hurt them. Why don't you just think about how they're going to feel? Maybe that will help you change your mind. Also, I think it's dangerous business to start bothering them. You seem to be the kind of person who looks for trouble. I'm the kind of person who tries to avoid it.'' And so Donna once again swam away.

Sharpy then began swimming toward the swimmers. At first, no one saw his fin in the water. Then, as he got closer, someone saw his fin sticking out of the water and screamed, ''Shark! Shark! It's coming right at us!'' Immediately, everyone started running out of the water as fast as possible. When Sharpy saw what was happening, he started to laugh.

Then someone yelled, ''It's a great white shark. It's a

killer shark." After that, people started screaming even louder and this made Sharpy laugh even harder. The people in the water couldn't get out fast enough. They stumbled and fell. They ran and they crawled. They scraped themselves on the rocks. They tripped over one another. They were all scared that Sharpy would eat them.

Well, it didn't take long before all the people were out of the water. The water was empty, but the beach was crowded with people just looking out at Sharpy. Sharpy felt great. He was the center of attention and he had scared many people. He had had fun, he had gotten revenge, and nothing had happened to him.

So Sharpy swam away quite content. He didn't know, however, that at that very time the people on shore were having a meeting to decide what to do about Sharpy. Some suggested that they send out boats with guns, harpoons, and even explosives to try to kill him. Others, however, said that he was a very unusual shark, that great white sharks were very rare, and that they should try to catch him and put him in a big tank in the aquarium so that everyone could see him. Although they argued back and forth, all agreed that Sharpy must be stopped. Finally, the group that wished to capture him got more votes than the one that wished to kill him.

In the meantime, Donna again spoke with Sharpy, "That's a terrible thing you did to those people on the beach. I'm sure they're planning to do something to you, Sharpy. I think you'd better be very careful where you go and what you do."

"Aw, I don't have anything to worry about," said Sharpy.

"You don't seem to learn," said Donna. "You don't

seem to think in advance about consequences, about the things that will happen to you in return for what you do to others. You never seem to learn that when you harm others, they're likely to want to do things to stop you from harming them again. You still have the scars on your head from the boat motor. You still have the hole in your tail from the bullet. Yet these things don't help you remember that it's cruel to hurt others and that there are consequences." As Donna spoke, Sharpy hardly listened. He just kept thinking about the beach

scene and all the frightened people. So Donna swam away and thought to herself, "I feel sorry for him. I just know that terrible things are going to happen to him. He's cruel. He doesn't realize that he hurts others. He doesn't think about how others must feel when he's cruel to them. He doesn't think in advance about the consequences of what he does. And he doesn't seem to learn from his experiences. I just know that bad things are going to happen to him."

The next day, as Sharpy was swimming and searching for food, he smelled and tasted some blood in the water. He thought to himself, "There must be some good food around here with all this blood." He didn't know that men in a big steel boat had thrown bloody meat and fish in the water in order to attract him. Sharpy swam toward the place from which the smell and taste was coming. Soon he saw globs of meat and fish in the water and he began gobbling them up.

Sharpy was having a great feast and didn't think about where all this good food might be coming from.

Sharpy didn't know that some of the globs of meat and fish had big hooks in them and that the hooks were attached to steel wires that were connected to machines on the boat. They weren't attached to fishing rods, because a great white shark is too big and strong to be caught by one man or even a few men holding a fishing rod.

Suddenly, Sharpy bit one of the pieces of meat that was on a hook. When he chewed on the meat, the hook went into the side of his mouth. When he tried to spit it out, it wouldn't go. It was stuck in his mouth. Then he felt the wire pull him toward the boat. Sharpy started to swim away in the other direction. However, as big and as strong as he was, and as hard as he tried, the boat was stronger. The boat then started to move toward the shore and Sharpy was dragged behind it. This time the people on the boat were not crying out in fear. They were shouting with joy.

As they moved along in the water, the machine that was pulling Sharpy began rolling in the wire. Sharpy got pulled closer and closer to the boat. And, no matter how hard he tried, he couldn't stop the machine from pulling him in and he couldn't stop the boat from pulling him toward the shore. Harder and harder he pulled and closer and closer he was dragged to the boat. Finally, he was pulled up right to the edge of the boat. Sharpy was very angry and very scared. He wondered whether the men would kill him.

Suddenly Sharpy felt a loop of steel wire around his tail. He tried to shake it off but he couldn't. The more he squirmed, the tighter it became. Now Sharpy was caught at both ends. A hook in his mouth and a loop around his tail. Although he was still thrashing around, he didn't know what was going to happen to him next.

But it didn't take long for Sharpy to find out. Suddenly he felt himself being lifted out of the water. You can imagine how scared he was then. The machine

lifted him into the air by the hook in his mouth while the men held on to the loop around his tail. Then the machine turned and lowered him into a big water tank that was on the deck of the boat. Although Sharpy was still petrified, he was relieved to be in water again.

As soon as he was lowered into the tank, the men lowered a big steel cover on the top and clamped it down. There were holes in it, through which Sharpy could see what was going on above. And the main thing he saw was the faces of the men looking down at him in the tank. They were cheering and laughing at the same time.

Sharpy was trapped. No matter how hard he thrashed, he couldn't get out of the tank. After some time, he started to get tired and so stopped jumping around. Even if he were not tired and even if he had still jumped around, it wouldn't have done him any good. The tank was much too strong for him. As Sharpy lay there exhausted, he wondered what the men would do to him. He was sorry now that he had caused all this trouble. And he started to realize that he was responsible for much, if not all, of the trouble.

After what seemed like a very long ride, the boat
finally reached the shore. When it came to the dock,
there was a big crowd of people cheering. Everyone was
happy that Sharpy was caught. Everyone but Sharpy,
of course. As they tied up to the dock, Sharpy heard

people shouting, "Kill him. Kill him. Let's get rid of
him forever." You can imagine how scared Sharpy was
when he heard this.

But then one of the men on the boat said, "No,
we're taking him to the aquarium. We're going to put

him in a big glass tank there so that everyone can see him. He's a rare one. It's not every day that we catch a great white shark.''

So Sharpy was put in the big glass tank in the aquarium. Every day the people came to look at him. Although Sharpy was happy to be alive, his life in the aquarium was very sad. Although he could swim around in the tank, it was nothing like the big wide

ocean, so he always felt cramped. Although he never had to worry about getting food again, he would have much preferred the freedom of the big wide ocean. Over the years, as he swam around the tank, he thought many, many times of the things that Donna the Dolphin had said to him. He missed her very much and realized that she was very wise. He was very sorry that he had ignored her advice. And Donna was sorry, as well, when she heard from the other fish what had happened to Sharpy.

Lessons:

1) Think about other people's feelings if you're planning to make fun of, scare, or bother them.

2) Treat other people the same way you would like them to treat you. Or, as the old saying goes, "Do unto others as you would have others do unto you."

The Squirrel and the Nuts

Once there was a squirrel named Sandy. When she was very young, her mother said to her and her brothers and her sisters, "Children, I want to tell you something very important, something that I want you to remember for the rest of your lives."

"What's that?" said the children. "It must be very important if you're so serious about it."

"As you know, children, we have a lot of nuts and seeds here in the forest where we live. That's because it's summertime now and the weather is warm. But it will not always be this way. Before long, the weather will get cooler. The color of the leaves will change from green to red and yellow and brown. It will then be autumn. And after that the weather will get even colder and white snow will fall on the ground. It will then be winter. In the winter, it will not only be very cold, but we won't be able to find seeds, and nuts, and other foods. Therefore, we must save up some of our food and store it away for the winter. We can eat *some* of our food now, but we *must save* some for the winter or else we may all starve."

All the brothers and sisters thought that what their mother had said made good sense. All except Sandy. Sandy said to herself, "I'll worry about the winter when the winter comes. Now it's summer and I'm going to enjoy myself." And so, during the summer and fall all of the other squirrels did two

things. They ate some of their nuts and seeds and they saved some for winter. They hid their food in holes in trees and buried some in the ground. But Sandy did

only one thing. She just ate all of her food and saved none.

When the autumn came and the leaves started to turn into many pretty colors, the other squirrels began saving even more nuts and seeds. They knew that the cold winter would soon be here and they wanted to be sure that they had enough to eat, but Sandy continued to live in her world of dreams. "I'll worry about winter when winter comes," she said. "In the meantime, I'm going to enjoy the beautiful autumn weather."

Finally the winter came and the snow began to fall. Like all the other squirrels, Sandy crawled into a hole in a tree for protection from the cold, the wind, the ice, and the snow. You know, of course, what the big

difference was between Sandy's home and that of the
other squirrels. Sandy's hole was empty. The holes of
the other squirrels were filled with nuts, seeds, and
other foods.

Now Sandy was very sad. Now she was sorry that she
hadn't planned ahead and thought about what would

happen in the winter. Now she was sorry that she had
only thought of the present, and not the future.

Sandy then went around to the other squirrels and
asked them for food. Most of them told her that they
wouldn't give her any. They told her that it wasn't fair
that she had sat around all summer and fall doing
nothing and now she wanted them to feed her. A few
of the other squirrels gave her just a little bit of food,
but none of them gave her a lot. And none of them
gave her their best seeds and nuts either. All squirrels,
however, told her that she really didn't deserve to get
any nuts and seeds because she had been so lazy.

And so Sandy started to search for food under the
cold ice and snow. It was not only a lot of hard work,
but she suffered much because of the cold and wind. In
addition, because it was winter, there was very little

food to be found. The little bit she was able to find was that which had been left over from the summer and fall.

And so all winter long Sandy went on like this. When she begged food from others, she only got a little bit. Even then she felt ashamed of herself, especially when the others called her names like "lazy" and "good-for-nothing." And when she hunted for food she suffered from the cold and the long hours of searching.

Finally the spring came and the weather started to get warm again. Sandy knew that the nuts and seeds and other foods would soon start to grow again and then her suffering would be over.

She knew, as well, that she had learned her lesson and that she would never again make the mistake of not thinking ahead about what things were going to happen the next winter. She would never again make the mistake of just thinking about the present and not about the future as well.

And that's exactly what happened that year, and the next year, and the next. Sandy was very careful to save some of the food she found in the spring and summer so that she would have enough to eat in the winter.

Lessons:
1) Plan ahead.
2) Learn from your mistakes.

The Ostrich and the Lion

Once there was a lion. Her name was Linda. She was still young and spent lots of time playing with the other girl and boy lion cubs. One day, as they were playing, a group of ostriches passed them in a nearby field. "What are those?" said Linda to one of the other lions.

"They're ostriches," said the other lion. "I met a man once who told me a very strange thing about ostriches. He said that most human beings believe that ostriches hide their heads in the sand when there's danger. I don't know whether it's true or not, but it certainly sounds strange. I know that we lions would never do such a foolish thing."

Linda also thought that that was a foolish thing for an ostrich to do and wondered whether it was really true. Linda had heard that human beings believe all kinds of strange and even crazy things, and she wondered whether this was another one of those ideas. Anyway, the ostriches passed and Linda returned to playing with her friends.

One day, while playing hide-and-seek with her friends, Linda went to hide deep in the jungle. She waited a long time for someone to come and try to find her, but nothing happened. She could hear the voices of the other lions in the distance and she knew that there was nothing to be afraid of. And so she remained hidden. As she waited for someone to find her, Linda began to daydream. She thought about all kinds of pleasant things: the good times she had had with her mother and father, the fun times she had with her friends, and the enjoyable times she often had when she was alone.

Linda didn't realize how long she was daydreaming. When she finally realized how much time she had spent daydreaming, she could no longer hear the voices of the other lions. Linda immediately got up and started running toward the place where the lions had been playing. As she ran, she called out the names of her friends. But no one answered. And when she got there, no one was around. They had all left.

Linda started to get very frightened. She didn't know the way they had gotten to the place in the jungle where they had played hide-and-seek. And she didn't know the way back to the den where she lived with her family. So Linda decided to guess the way back. She walked for a while in one direction and the jungle

looked ever stranger. Then she turned and walked in
another direction. Again, things looked very strange.
Linda wandered around longer and longer and still
couldn't find anything that looked familiar. Finally she
had to accept the fact that she was lost. She was very
hungry and thirsty and became more frightened than
ever.

As she sat there wondering what to do, Linda decided
that first she had to get something to eat and drink.
She was very, very thirsty and very, very hungry. In the
distance, she heard what sounded like the babbling
waters of a brook. She followed the sound and, sure
enough, there was a brook. She quickly ran over to the
brook and drank as much water as she could drink.
Although she was no longer thirsty, she was still quite
hungry. As she was thinking about how she would get
something to eat, she heard some strange sounds. She
thought that she had heard such sounds before, but
couldn't remember where or when. So Linda followed
the sounds and, before long, she came to a large field.
There she saw some ostriches. "Great," said Linda to

herself, "now I'm going to have something good to eat. This should be easy, because when they see me they'll probably just put their heads in the sand, like the man told my friend."

So Linda peered through the jungle bushes and watched the ostriches. She tried to pick out which one she was going to catch and eat. While she was doing this, she didn't know that the ostriches had seen her. The first thing the ostriches did when they saw Linda was to crouch down on their bellies in such a way that their bodies were hidden in the tall grass. But they lay in such a way that they could still look at Linda through spaces between the blades of grass.

When Linda saw what the ostriches were doing she thought that the man was right and that they were hiding their heads in the sand. She didn't know that she was being watched very carefully so that the ostriches could decide whether to fight her or run away. She didn't know that even though ostriches can't fly very high or far, they can run very fast. In fact, the ostrich is probably the fastest running of all the birds. She didn't know also that ostriches have very sharp claws and very powerful legs that can make them very dangerous animals to fight with.

When Linda decided which ostrich she wanted to eat, she suddenly leaped out of the bushes. The ostrich, however, did not have her head in the sand as Linda had thought. She was fully prepared for Linda and started to run. But Linda had leaped too quickly and the ostrich couldn't run away. Linda sunk her teeth

deeply into the ostrich's leg. As Linda's teeth sunk into the ostrich's leg, the ostrich cried out so loudly that Linda became frightened. Then the ostrich started scratching Linda's body with the claws of her other foot. The claws went deep into Linda's back and they were very painful. Linda tried hard to hold onto the ostrich's other leg. But the blows from the ostrich's free leg were very, very hard and more and more blood kept flowing from the deep gashes the ostrich's claws were making in Linda's back. Finally, Linda could stand it no longer and she let go of the ostrich. She then ran away as fast as she could and the ostrich ran in the opposite direction. And it's hard to say who ran away faster!

When Linda got back to the jungle she was very, very tired and, of course, even more hungry. As she lay there, catching her breath, she thought, "Well, that's just another example of the silly things many human beings believe. Ostriches don't hide their heads in the sand when there's trouble. Maybe humans are foolish enough to do something like that, but ostriches certainly aren't."

As Linda lay there wondering what she was going to do next, she suddenly heard in the distance the voices of her friends. They were calling out her name and were still looking for her. Linda jumped up and ran toward them, all the time calling out their names as well. You can imagine how happy they all were to see one another.

Of course, everyone asked Linda what had happened to her and how she had gotten wounded so badly. While eating supper, Linda told them the whole story. They were happy to see that her wounds would heal and to know that she was going to be all right. They

were happy, as well, to have learned the important lesson that ostriches would never do such a stupid thing as put their heads in the sand when there was danger. They learned that the ostrich either fights or runs away, just like all the other animals in the forest and jungle. And they agreed with Linda that human beings probably are silly enough to do a thing like that and to believe that ostriches would do such a foolish thing as well.

Lessons:
1) Ostriches would never do such a stupid thing as hold their heads in the sand when there's danger. They either fight or run away, just like all the other animals.
2) Human beings may be the only animals who make believe that there's no trouble when there really is.

The Beaver
and
the Owl

Deep in the forest there lived some beavers. Beavers, as you may know, are very hard workers. That is why people sometimes say that a person is as "busy as a beaver." One of the reasons why beavers work so hard is that they build dams. These dams are made from wooden logs, twigs, stone, and mud. The dams slow down the water in streams and make good places for the beavers to live and have their children. They also protect beavers from animals who might want to harm them.

Beavers have very long sharp teeth with which they can slowly bite off logs and twigs from trees. The beavers then drag these logs to the stream and pile them up with mud and stones until they have a dam. It takes a long time to build a dam and it's not easy because the water may wash the logs downstream.

Although the beaver gets the wood on the land, he can live under the water. There aren't too many animals who can live both on land and under water. That's one of the reasons why the beaver is such an interesting animal.

In the part of the forest that I am now talking about, there lived a beaver named Beverly. Her friends called her Bev. Bev was a very hard working beaver. In fact, she was generally busier and harder working than most of the other beavers. And because beavers work so hard anyway, that wasn't an easy thing to do.

In one of the trees in the same part of the forest that I am talking about there lived an owl named Oliver.

Oliver was very smart. He was very old and had learned many useful things in his time. He used to like watching all the different animals in the forest and had learned many useful things over the years. He was so wise that many animals used to come to him for advice.

One day, the beavers with whom Bev lived decided to build a new dam. The group was getting too big for all of them to fit in the dam where they were living. So they decided to look at the different parts of the stream and see which one would be the best place for the new dam. Most of the beavers decided that the place near the old oak would be the best. But Bev and some of her friends thought that the place near the big rock would be better. Most of the other beavers, especially the older ones, agreed that there would be more space near the big rock, but they said that the stream would be too wide and swift to build a dam there.

And so each group began building at its favorite place. Things went quite well for the bigger and older group, the group of beavers that was building near the old oak tree. There, because the stream moved slowly, the logs remained in place long enough to stick in the mud and stones.

Bev's group, however, was having trouble. The stream was swift and many logs broke away. But the more the logs broke away, the more Bev tried to build a dam. Her friends were getting very tired and upset. They were also getting very discouraged. One of them suggested that they seek the advice of Oliver, the wise old owl. All agreed. And so they went to Oliver and told him the problem. Oliver then said, "If at first you don't succeed, try, try again." That was the way Oliver used to give advice. He usually said something very short.

But it was usually very wise even though she didn't give a long, involved explanation.

And so Bev and her friends went back to the dam and started working harder. Although they got further, they still had much trouble. The stream was really quite swift where they were working and many of the logs still got washed downstream. Bev's friends got more and more upset and more and more discouraged.

One of Bev's friends thought it might be a good idea to seek again advice from the wise old owl. And so they all went again and told the owl that they were still having trouble. Then the wise old owl said, "If at first you don't succeed, try, try again. If after that, you still don't succeed, forget it. Don't make a big fool of yourself!"

All of Bev's friends thought that this was very good advice and they decided to quit working on the dam. But not Bev. She insisted that it could be done, and if the others weren't going to help her, she'd do it herself. The others thought that this was very silly, because beavers have to work together as a team to build a dam. It was hard enough building it with others; building a dam alone was much harder, if not impossible. And to build this particular dam alone would certainly be impossible. So the other beavers returned to the old oak tree and saw that the new dam was already completed. Bev, however, stayed and continued to try to complete the dam.

Things then got even worse for Bev after that. The harder she seemed to work, the less success she had. More and more logs broke away and there was no one to help her catch them. Instead of getting bigger, her dam was getting smaller—even though she was busier than ever. Every once in a while the others came by to see how Bev was doing. And when they saw how foolish Bev was being, and how stubborn she was, they started to laugh at her. But even this didn't stop her. She still kept trying. Bev was very stubborn. Bev

wouldn't give up hope even though everyone else thought that the task was hopeless.

Finally, Bev decided to seek again advice from the wise old owl. Again the wise old owl said, "If at first you don't succeed, try, try again. If after that, you still don't succeed, forget it. Don't make a big fool of yourself."

"Don't you have any other advice than that?" said Bev. "I think that advice is silly."

"It's not as silly as you think, young lady," said the wise old owl. "If you slow down enough to think about it a while, you may find it to be very wise and useful indeed. It's too bad that there aren't more people around who follow this advice."

Bev walked away very angry. "'...If after that you

still don't succeed, forget it.' How stupid," she said to herself. "'Don't make a big fool of yourself.' That's foolish," she kept saying to herself. Over and over again Bev kept saying what the wise old owl had told her. And over and over again she kept saying that the old owl's advice was silly.

When Bev got back to the dam, she started trying again. And as she worked, the owl's words kept repeating themselves in her head. And as she worked, more and more logs kept floating downstream. As she watched the logs floating away, Bev slowly began to realize that the owl's words weren't as silly as she had first thought. Finally, she said to herself, "I hate to admit it, but the old bird's right: 'If after that, you still don't succeed, forget it. Don't make a big fool of yourself.'" And so Bev finally quit. Then she returned to the place where the other beavers were and admitted that she had been stubborn and wrong. It was hard for her to say that she had been wrong, but she couldn't deny that she had been. And they all congratulated her on being brave enough to admit that she had made a big mistake.

Lessons:
1) If at first you don't succeed, try, try again. If after that, you still don't succeed, forget it. Don't make a big fool of yourself.
2) To admit mistakes is brave; to cover them up is cowardly.
3) You get more respect when you admit mistakes than when you deny them.

The Fox *
and
the Big Lie

Once there was a fox named Dick. From the time he was very young, the thing he wanted most in the whole world was to be king of all the other foxes in the large forest where he lived. This forest was so huge that there were thousands and thousands of foxes who lived there. The fox who became their king was a powerful person indeed.

*Any similarity between the foxes depicted in this story and any other foxes, living or dead, is purely coincidental.

In order to become king of all the foxes in the forest, he first had to become chief of a small den of foxes in the part of the forest where he lived. All the foxes voted in an election for the fox they wished to be their leader. The fox who was elected was called the *den chief.* The next step toward being king was to become leader of all the den chiefs in a larger part of the forest. All the den chiefs voted in an election and the winner was called a *group chief.* The last and final step toward becoming king was to be elected by all the group chiefs. All the group chiefs competed with one another to become *king of the forest.*

As I'm sure you can imagine, it was very hard to be elected king of the forest. In fact, it was very difficult being elected leader of any of the groups, whether it was den chief or group chief. The foxes who wanted to become chiefs would make speeches asking everyone to vote for them. Some of the foxes who wanted to be leaders told the truth about the things that they did and why they deserved to be elected. There were others, however, who told lies. They made up stories about the things they had done—things that had never happened. Or, they made promises they knew they could not keep. Sometimes the foxes who voted were fooled and believed what the liars had told them. Because of this, the liars sometimes got elected and the honest foxes didn't. This, I'm sure you will agree, was a very sad thing.

Now Dick was one of the liars. In fact, he was one of the biggest liars of them all. Whenever someone tried to prove that he had lied, Dick either denied it or made up an excuse. Often, he would make a speech in which he

tried to get people to believe he hadn't done the wrong thing. At other times he'd make a speech asking people to forgive him. But even in these speeches he never admitted the biggest lies, only the smallest ones. After a while, people started calling him "slippery" because no one could prove that he was lying. He was like a slippery fish that no one could catch. Some people started calling him "Slippery Dick." Others called him "Tricky Dick" because of the tricky things he did to cover up his lies. They also called him Tricky Dick because of the many sneaky things he did.

Even though lots of people called him Slippery Dick and Tricky Dick, thousands of foxes still liked him. And even though most people knew about his big lies, thousands of people still voted for him. Many didn't want to hear about the lies. There were some who even admired him for the fact that he could lie and get away without being punished.

Dick was very clever—clever enough to get elected den chief when he was very young. Then, when he got a little older, he got enough people to believe that he

was a good guy that he was elected group chief of all the den chiefs in the part of the forest where he lived. In Dick's mind, these victories were just steps toward becoming king of all the foxes in the forest. The first time Dick tried to be elected king, he lost the election. Too many people remembered what a big liar he was and so they didn't vote for him. However, eight years later, Dick decided to run again to be elected king. He hoped that by this time people would have forgotten all the lies and the other sneaky things he had done. And that is exactly what happened. So many people forgot what he had done, and so many believed his new lies, that he was elected king. The people who knew what a fake he was were very upset that a crook could be elected king. But there was nothing they could do about it.

You might think that now that Dick was finally king, he would stop doing tricky and sneaky things. But he didn't. It was almost as if he didn't know how to act any other way. It was almost as if he had been lying so long that he didn't know how to tell the truth any more.

One day, some foxes who were friends of Dick tried to steal some chickens from a farmer's chicken coop. However, they were caught as they tried to get away with the chickens. Everybody knew that they were friends of Dick and that they were stealing the chickens for him. But Dick, as was expected, denied that he had asked these foxes to steal the chickens for him. Dick then made up more and more lies trying to convince people that he knew nothing about the crime. The more

Dick lied, the more people tried to prove that Dick knew about it and had told his friends to steal the chickens.

So back and forth it went. More and more proof was found that showed that Dick knew about the crime and that he had actually asked his friends to steal the chickens for him. More and more Dick lied and told his friends to lie in order to cover up the fact that he was involved. And the more Dick tried to cover up, the angrier the other foxes became. The more Dick tried to cover up, the greater was the number of foxes who began to doubt him. Finally, even his closest friends no longer could fool themselves into believing that he was telling the truth. By this time, there was practically no one who believed a word he said, and so he could no longer rule the forest. His best friends then came to him and told him that if he didn't quit as king, all the group chiefs and the den chiefs were going to get together and vote him out of office.

So Dick decided to quit. Dick quit in disgrace, with

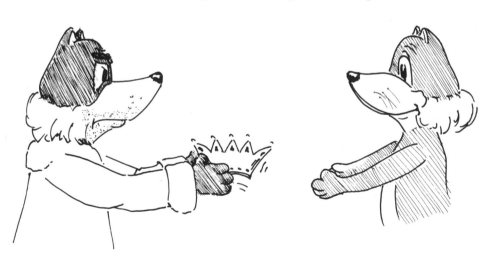

everyone scorning him and everyone being angry at him.

You would think that after losing his kingdom Dick would have learned his lesson. You would think that after that Dick would have finally admitted that he had been involved in the crime and that he had lied and tried to cover this up. But no! He still went around telling everybody that he was innocent. Hardly anyone believed him. Actually, many people felt sorry for him.

Hardly anyone respected him and, worst of all, he didn't even like himself. And so for the rest of his life Dick kept going around telling everyone that he was honest. Hardly anyone believed him, but they were too polite to tell him this to his face.

Of course, it would have been much better if Dick had never started to lie in the first place. And, of course, it would have been better if Dick had not told his friends to steal chickens for him in the first place.

But once everybody knew about the crime, it would have been much better if he had admitted that the thieves were working under his orders. It would have been much better if he had admitted that he had made a mistake. Had he done this, he probably would have gotten very little, if any, punishment. This was especially so because he was the king. By trying to cover up the wrong things that he had done, he made things worse for himself. By trying to cover up and lie about what he had done, he made a new and *bigger* problem for himself that just made things much worse.

And that is the story of Tricky Dick, the sly fox, who ended up fooling himself more than anyone else! And he lived out his life a sad and lonely man.

Lessons:
1) Try not to lie.
2) Try not to do bad things.
3) If you do lie or if you do bad things, it's best to admit it. Then you'll probably just get one small punishment for what you did.
4) If you try to cover up the bad things you do, you may create much bigger problems for yourself. You'll probably get much bigger punishments— both for having done the wrong thing and for having covered up.
5) Honesty is the best policy.